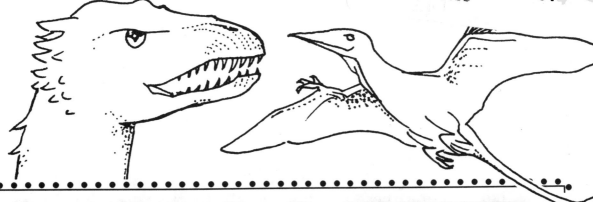

DINOSAUR DOTS

Monica Russo

Sterling Publishing Co., Inc.　New York

Acknowledgments

The facts and figures in these pages came from many sources. I used numerous books for reference, especially those by Edwin Colbert, John Horner, David Norman, and Helen Sattler, to name only a few. I found the books of Robert Bakker and Gregory Paul—with some of the latest concepts and controversies—to be very helpful. I would like to thank these authors and all the other geologists, paleontologists, and rock-readers around the world who have shared with the rest of us their amazing discoveries. I also give thanks and respect to the Earth's resources and the eons of Time, for producing the stony records of our past that may someday also show us our future.

© 1991 by Monica Russo
Published by Sterling Publishing Company, Inc.
387 Park Avenue South, New York, N.Y. 10016
Distributed in Canada by Sterling Publishing
% Canadian Manda Group, P.O. Box 920, Station U
Toronto, Ontario, Canada M8Z 5P9
Distributed in Great Britain and Europe by Cassell PLC
Villiers House, 41/47 Strand, London WC2N 5JE, England
Distributed in Australia by Capricorn Ltd.
P.O. Box 665, Lane Cove, NSW 2066
Manufactured in the United States of America
All rights reserved

Sterling ISBN 0-8069-7388-9 Paper

About the Creatures in This Book

The prehistoric animals in this book were drawn with a little imagination and a lot of information. We can only guess at how large dinosaurs were and what they weighed. Why? Different fossils of the same dinosaur have been found in different sizes, for one thing. A dinosaur's weight might have changed during the course of a year, just the way ours can. Male and female dinosaurs of the same type might have been different in size and weight. No one knows. We tried, though, to give you the latest information that most scientists will agree upon.

We also may never know what the colors and patterns of dinosaurs were like. They may have been bright yellow, blue, green or red, like some modern birds and lizards. Camouflage colors like dull green and brown would have helped conceal plant-eating dinosaurs. But fossils cannot tell us what the colors of the dinosaurs were, so use your imagination when you color these animals. You can add stripes, spots or blotches, just like the ones on modern animals. Have fun with them!

Name:	Albertosaurus
How to say it:	al BER toe SAW ris
Size:	About 28 feet (8.4m) long
It weighed about two tons (1.8 tonnes).
What it ate:	Meat
When it lived:	65 to 75 million years ago
Fossils have been found in:	Alberta, Canada

Albertosaurus

Albertosaurus probably looked like a small Tyrannosaurus (see page 94).

It used to be called Gorgosaurus (GOR go SAW ris).

Name:	Allosaurus
How to say it:	AL oh SAW ris
Size:	40 to 50 feet (12–15m) long About 15 feet (4.5m) tall
What it ate:	Meat
When it lived:	140 million years ago
Fossils have been found in:	Colorado, U.S.A.

Allosaurus   **Giraffe**

Allosaurus was pretty big, but it would have had to look up to a giraffe.

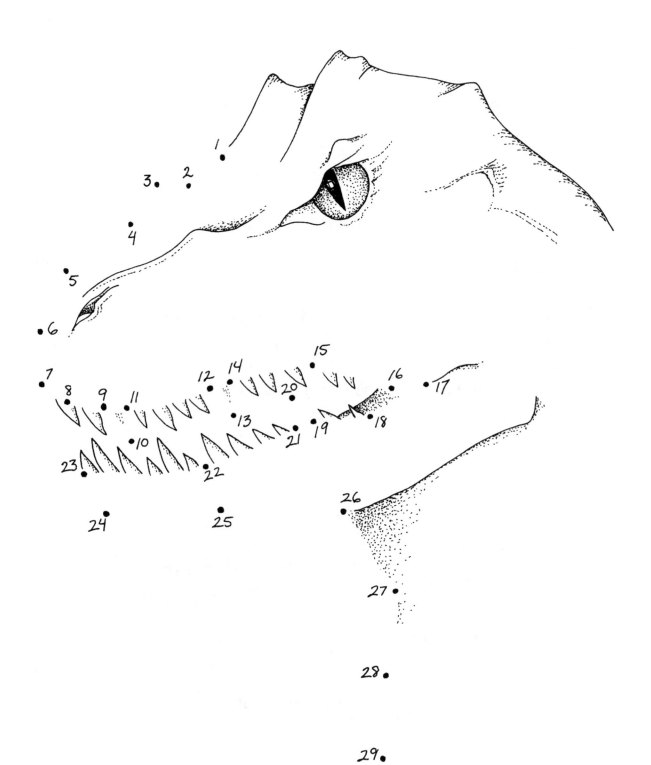

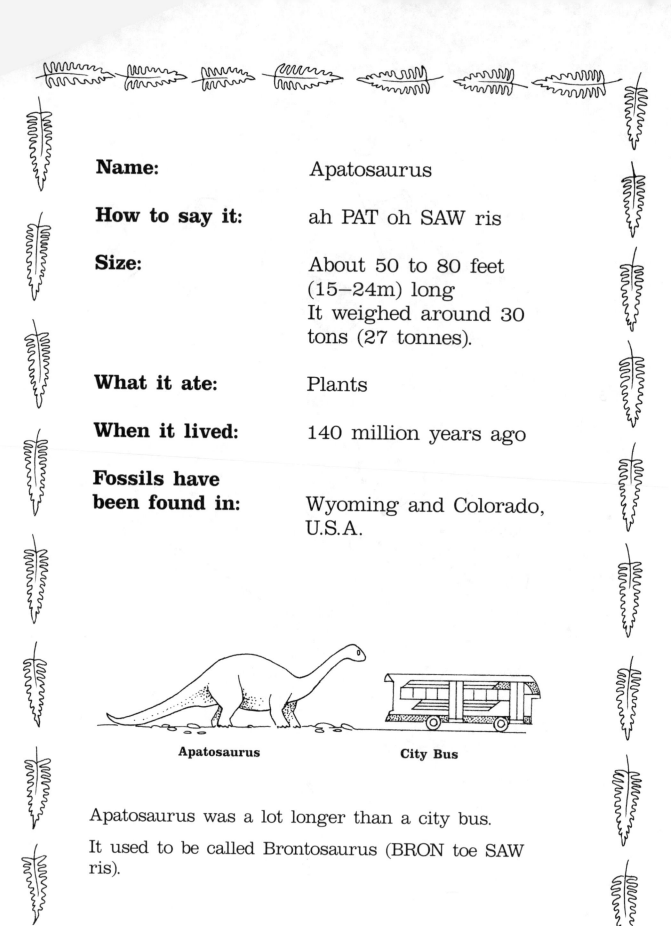

Name:	Apatosaurus
How to say it:	ah PAT oh SAW ris
Size:	About 50 to 80 feet (15–24m) long It weighed around 30 tons (27 tonnes).
What it ate:	Plants
When it lived:	140 million years ago
Fossils have been found in:	Wyoming and Colorado, U.S.A.

Apatosaurus   City Bus

Apatosaurus was a lot longer than a city bus.

It used to be called Brontosaurus (BRON toe SAW ris).

Name:	Archaeopteryx
How to say it:	arkee OP tiriks
Size:	About three feet (.9m) long
What it ate:	Insects and small animals
When it lived:	About 140 to 150 million years ago
Fossils have been found in:	Bavaria (Germany)

Archaeopteryx is often called "the First Bird."

Some scientists feel that this isn't a true dinosaur, because it looks too much like a bird.

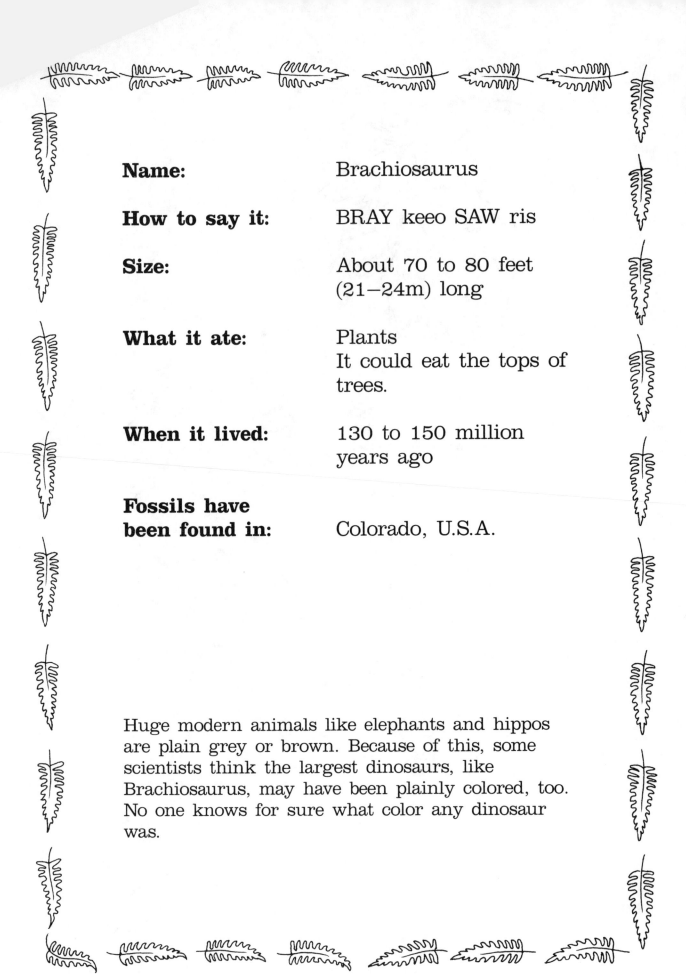

Name:	Brachiosaurus
How to say it:	BRAY keeo SAW ris
Size:	About 70 to 80 feet (21–24m) long
What it ate:	Plants It could eat the tops of trees.
When it lived:	130 to 150 million years ago
Fossils have been found in:	Colorado, U.S.A.

Huge modern animals like elephants and hippos are plain grey or brown. Because of this, some scientists think the largest dinosaurs, like Brachiosaurus, may have been plainly colored, too. No one knows for sure what color any dinosaur was.

13

Name:	Carnotaurus
How to say it:	KAR no TOR us
Size:	About 20 (6m) long
What it ate:	Meat
When it lived:	About 100 million years ago
Fossils have been found in:	Argentina, South America

Another name for this dinosaur is Carnotosaurus (kar NO toe SAW ris).

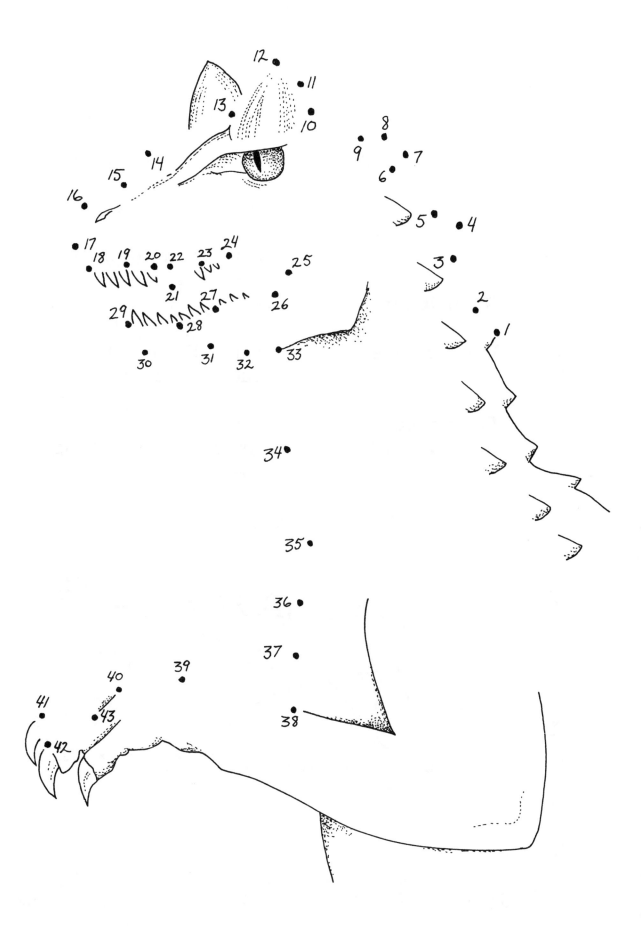

Name:	Ceratosaurus
How to say it:	SEER ah toe SAW ris or seer AH toe SAW ris
Size:	About 20 feet (6m) long
What it ate:	Meat
When it lived:	About 135 to 150 million years ago
Fossils have been found in:	Colorado and Wyoming, U.S.A.

These dinosaurs probably hunted in packs, as wolves do today.

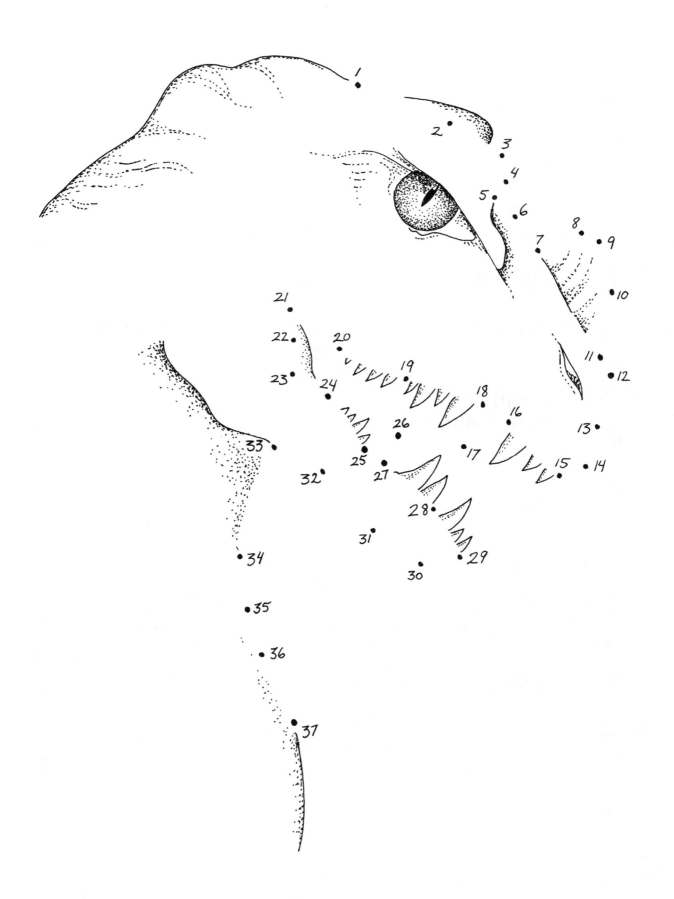

Name: Coelophysis

How to say it: SEE lo FY sis

Size: About seven to ten feet (2.1–3m) long

What it ate: Meat

When it lived: About 200 million years ago

Fossils have been found in: Arizona, U.S.A.

Coelophysis   Ostrich

Coelophysis was about as tall as an ostrich.

Name:	Compsognathus
How to say it:	KOMP so NAY this
Size:	Two to four feet (.6−1.2m) long
What it ate:	Insects, small lizards, small animals
When it lived:	About 140 to 145 million years ago
Fossils have been found in:	Germany and France

Compsognathus was small enough to curl up and sleep in a laundry basket.

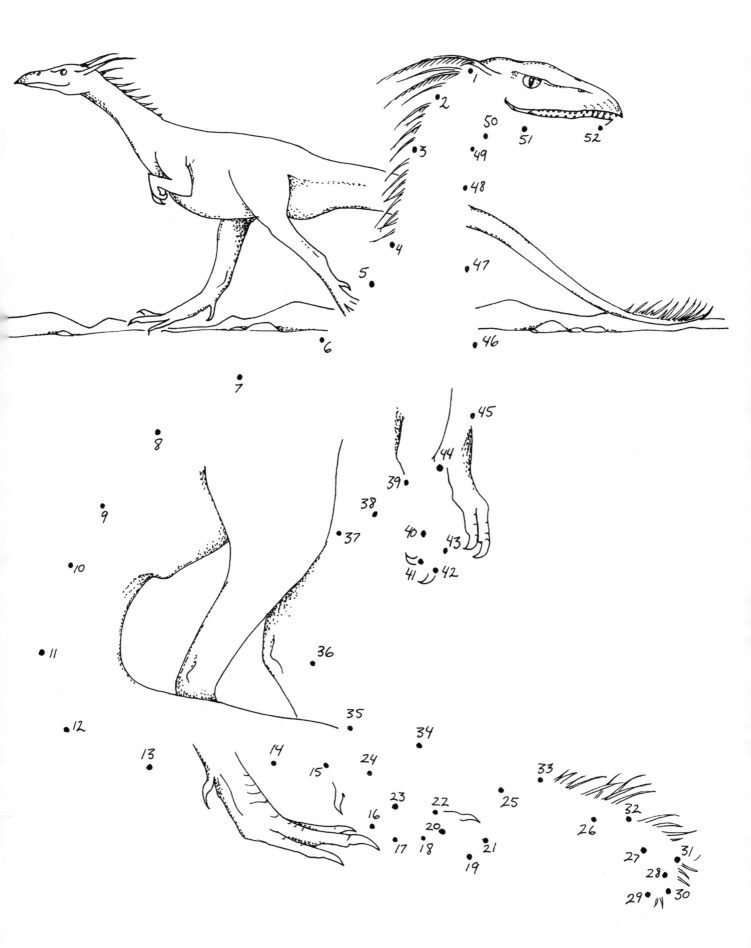

Name:	Corythosaurus
How to say it:	ko RITH ah SAW ris
Size:	About 33 feet (9.9m) long
What it ate:	Tough plants, like pine needles and twigs
When it lived:	About 75 to 95 million years ago
Fossils have been found in:	Alberta, Canada

There were more kinds of plant-eating dinosaurs than meat-eaters. The meat-eaters just get more attention!

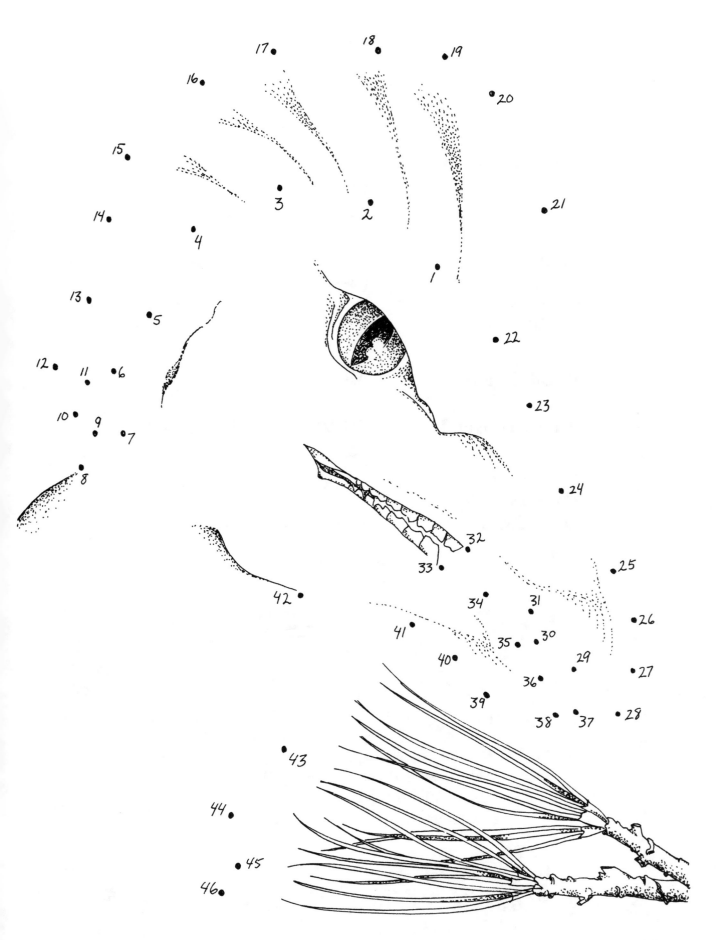

23

Name:	Deinonychus
How to say it:	DY no NIK us or dine ON ik us
Size:	About 10 to 13 feet (3–3.9m) long It was five feet (1.5m) tall.
What it ate:	Meat
When it lived:	70 to 100 million years ago
Fossils have been found in:	Montana, U.S.A.

Some scientists think this dinosaur may have had some feathers.

Name:	Dilophosaurus
How to say it:	dy LO fah SAW ris
Size:	About 20 feet (6m) long
What it ate:	Meat
When it lived:	About 180 to 190 million years ago
Fossils have been found in:	Arizona, U.S.A.

Dilophosaurus had weak jaws and probably hunted only for small animals.

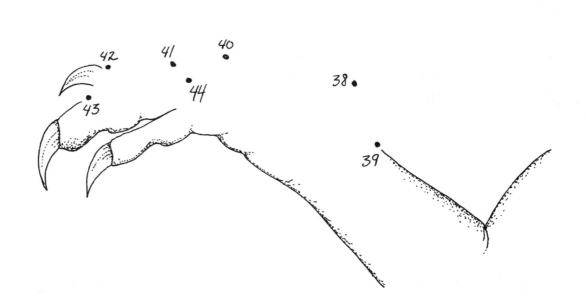

12
11
10
9
13
8
15 14
7
5 6
16
4
17
3
18
21 24
19 20 22 23 25
2
28
1
26
30 29 27
35
31
32 33
34
36
37
42 41 40
44 38
43
39

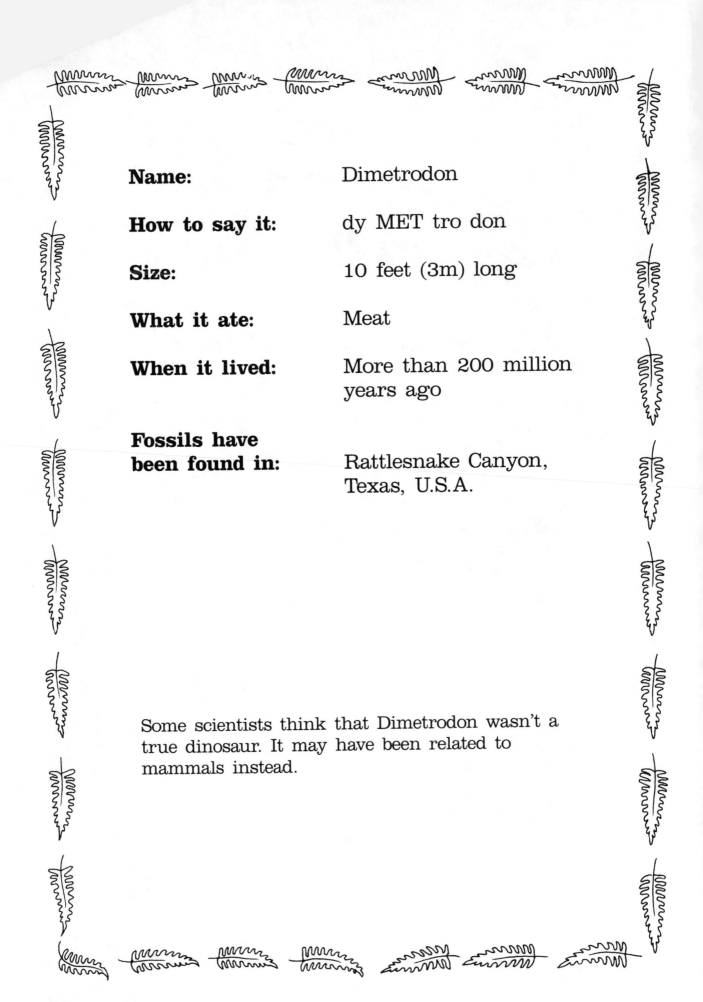

Name:	Dimetrodon
How to say it:	dy MET tro don
Size:	10 feet (3m) long
What it ate:	Meat
When it lived:	More than 200 million years ago
Fossils have been found in:	Rattlesnake Canyon, Texas, U.S.A.

Some scientists think that Dimetrodon wasn't a true dinosaur. It may have been related to mammals instead.

29

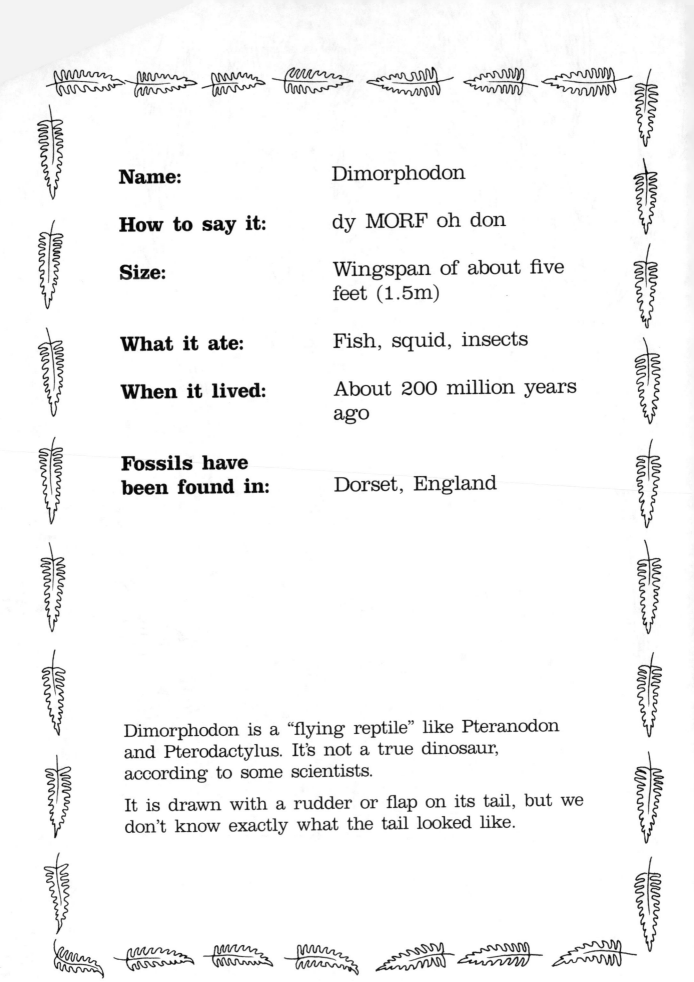

Name:	Dimorphodon
How to say it:	dy MORF oh don
Size:	Wingspan of about five feet (1.5m)
What it ate:	Fish, squid, insects
When it lived:	About 200 million years ago
Fossils have been found in:	Dorset, England

Dimorphodon is a "flying reptile" like Pteranodon and Pterodactylus. It's not a true dinosaur, according to some scientists.

It is drawn with a rudder or flap on its tail, but we don't know exactly what the tail looked like.

6 •   5 •

7 •
8 •

• 4

9 •

10 •

• 3

18 •

11 •   16   17

15 V V V V V V V
13   V   19
12 • V V 14 • 21 • 20 • 2 •
    24 • 22 •   1 •
25 • 23   26 • 27 • 28 •

29 •

30 •

31 •

31

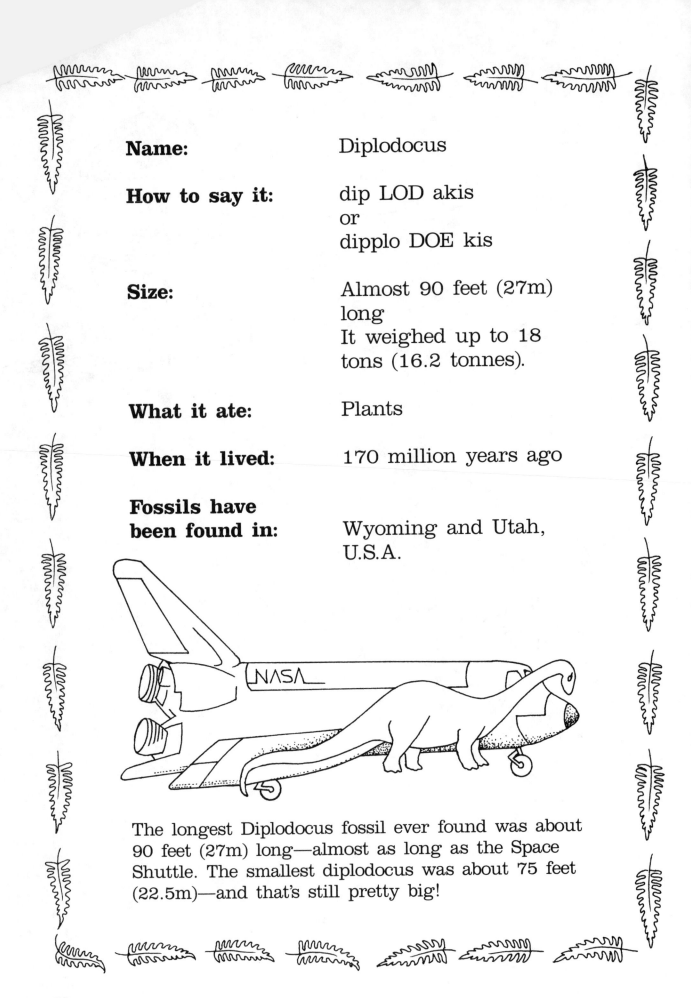

Name:	Diplodocus
How to say it:	dip LOD akis or dipplo DOE kis
Size:	Almost 90 feet (27m) long It weighed up to 18 tons (16.2 tonnes).
What it ate:	Plants
When it lived:	170 million years ago
Fossils have been found in:	Wyoming and Utah, U.S.A.

NASA

The longest Diplodocus fossil ever found was about 90 feet (27m) long—almost as long as the Space Shuttle. The smallest diplodocus was about 75 feet (22.5m)—and that's still pretty big!

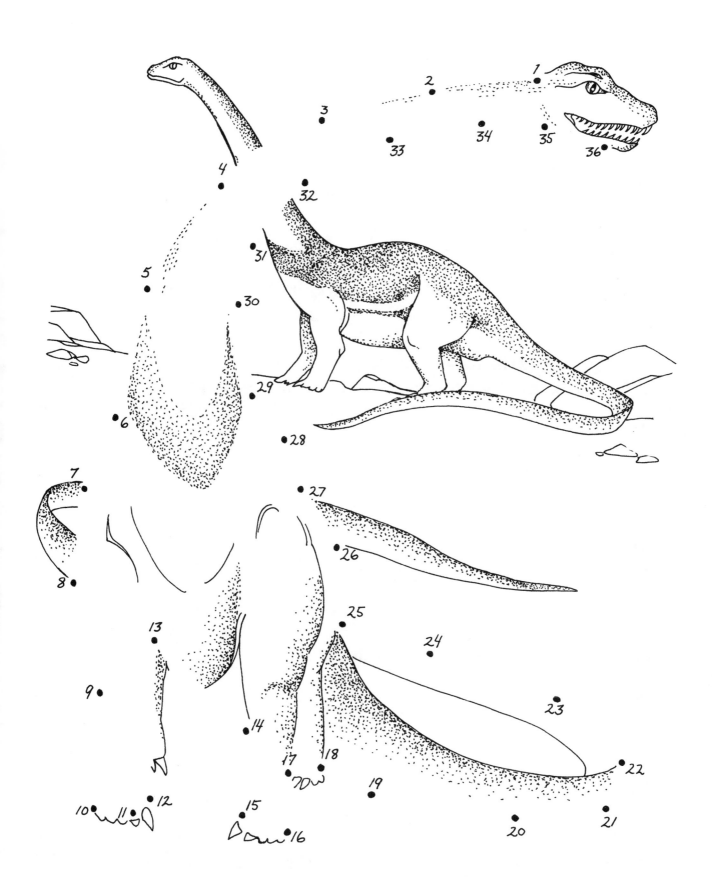

Name:	Edmontosaurus
How to say it:	ed MONT oh SAW ris
Size:	About 43 feet (12.9m) long
What it ate:	Leaves, fruits, seeds
When it lived:	About 65 to 90 million years ago
Fossils have been found in:	New Jersey and New Mexico, U.S.A. Alberta, Canada

Fossils of this dinosaur's skin show us it had scales on at least part of its body.

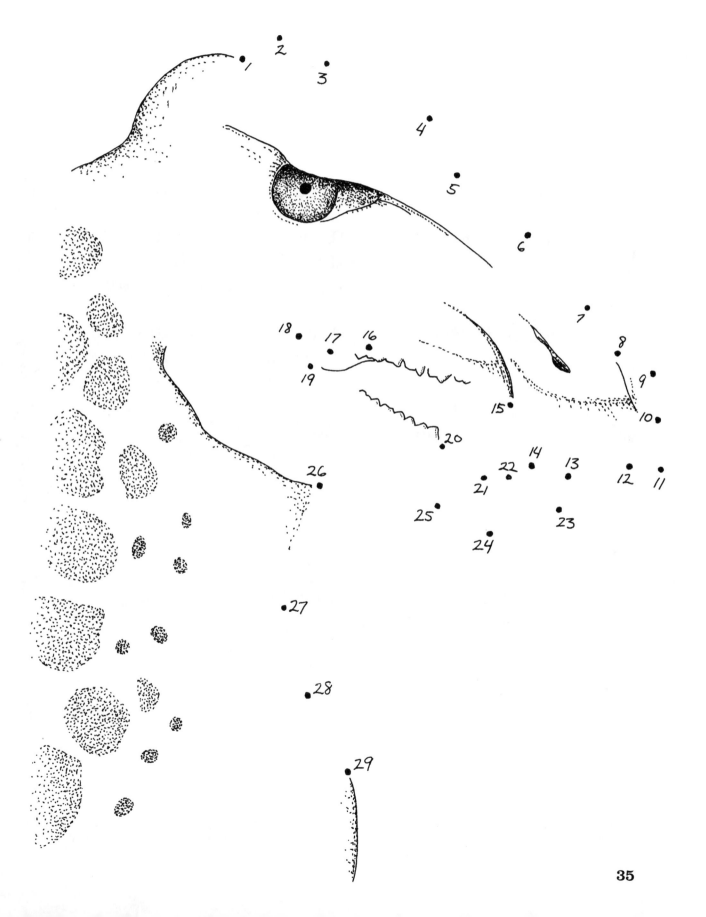

35

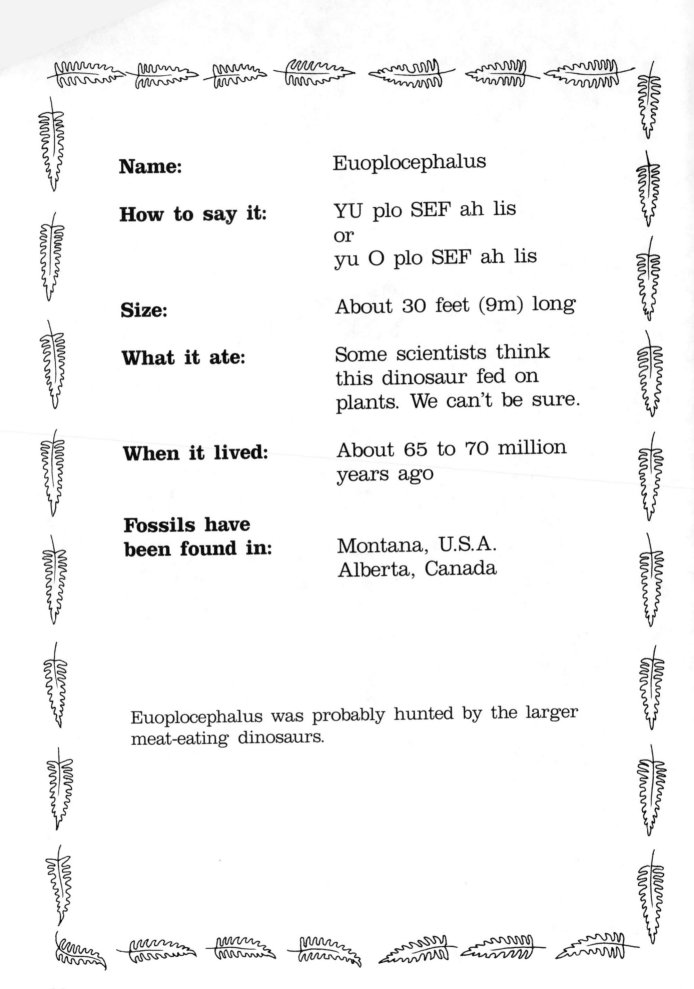

Name:	Euoplocephalus
How to say it:	YU plo SEF ah lis or yu O plo SEF ah lis
Size:	About 30 feet (9m) long
What it ate:	Some scientists think this dinosaur fed on plants. We can't be sure.
When it lived:	About 65 to 70 million years ago
Fossils have been found in:	Montana, U.S.A. Alberta, Canada

Euoplocephalus was probably hunted by the larger meat-eating dinosaurs.

Name:	Gallimimus
How to say it:	GAL ah MY mis
Size:	About 13 feet (3.9m) long
What it ate:	Some scientists think Gallimimus ate the eggs of other dinosaurs.
When it lived:	About 65 to 70 million years ago
Fossils have been found in:	Mongolia

Gallimimus had no teeth. It could have eaten eggs, and maybe insects, too.

Name:	Garudimimus
How to say it:	gah RU da MY mis
Size:	About 12 feet (3.6m) long
What it ate:	Eggs, insects, fruit
When it lived:	About 85 million years ago
Fossils have been found in:	Mongolia

Garudimimus had a bony ridge along the top of its beak. This ridge could have been the base for a flap of skin or row of long scales.

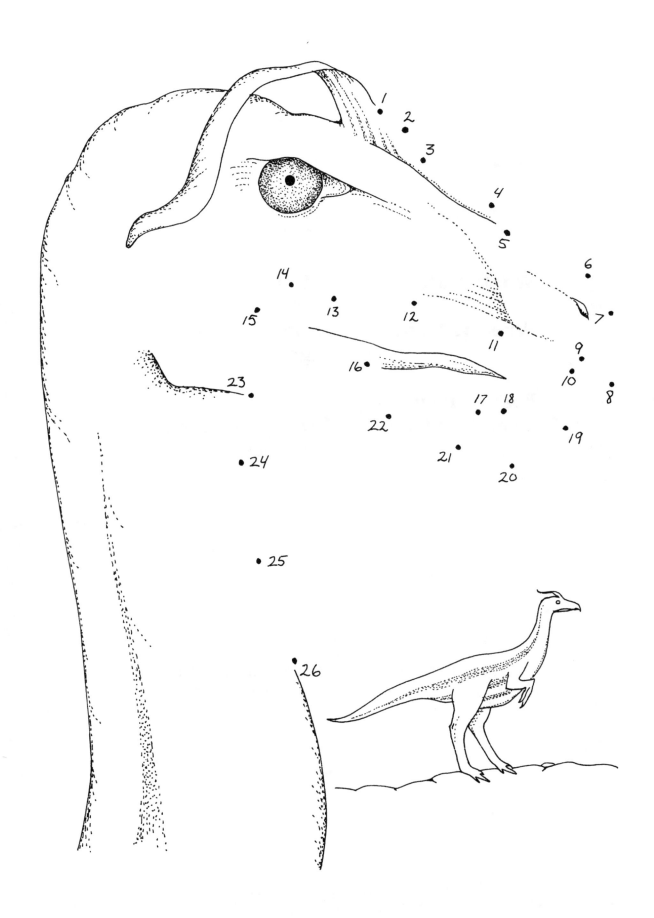

Name:	Herrerasaurus
How to say it:	Her AIR ah SAW ris
Size:	About six to eight feet (1.8–2.4m) long
What it ate:	Meat
When it lived:	About 230 million years ago
Fossils have been found in:	Argentina, South America

Since it had to hunt other animals for food, Herrerasaurus was probably a super-fast runner.

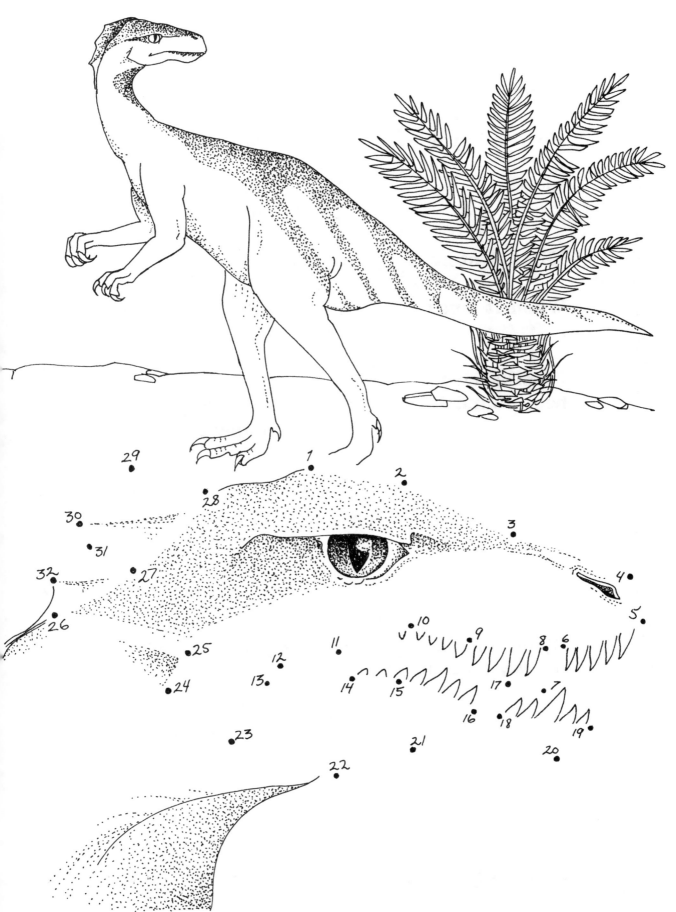

Name:	Hypacrosaurus
How to say it:	hy PAK rah SAW ris
Size:	From 18 to 25 feet (5.4–7.9m) long
What it ate:	Plants
When it lived:	About 70 to 80 million years ago
Fossils have been found in:	Montana, U.S.A. Alberta, Canada

Hypacrosaurus might have grazed on low plants, the way cows and sheep do today.

Name:	Hypsilophodon
How to say it:	HIP sih LOF oh don
Size:	About 4 to 6 feet (1.2–1.8m) long
What it ate:	Plants
When it lived:	About 110 million years ago
Fossils have been found in:	Isle of Wight, England

Hypsilophodon was short enough to walk in through your front door.

Name:	Ichthyosaurus
How to say it:	IK theeo SAW ris
Size:	About 10 feet (3m) long
What it ate:	Fish
When it lived:	More than 130 million years ago
Fossils have been found in:	Nevada, U.S.A.

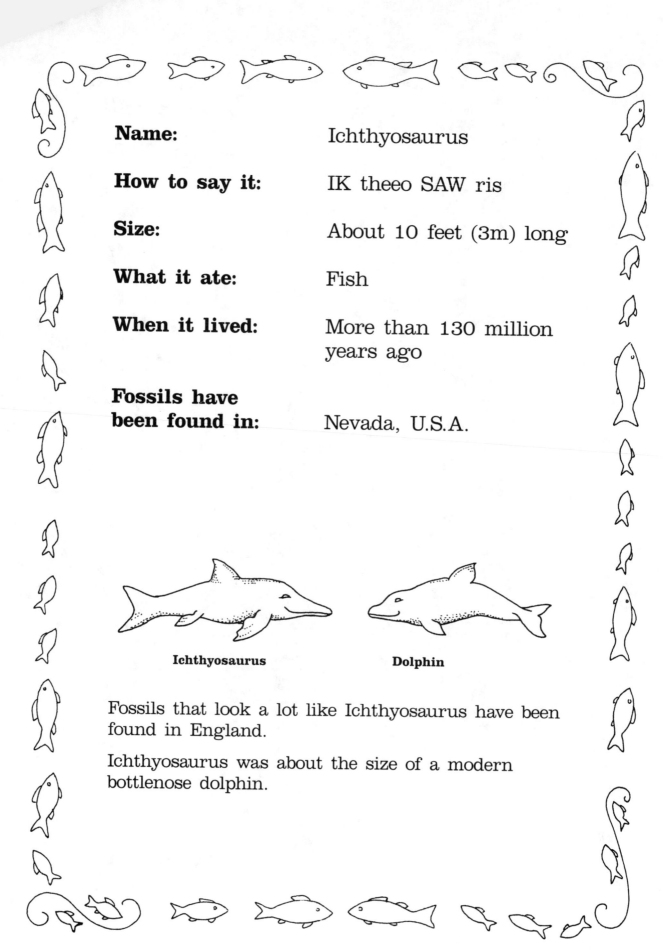

Ichthyosaurus   Dolphin

Fossils that look a lot like Ichthyosaurus have been found in England.

Ichthyosaurus was about the size of a modern bottlenose dolphin.

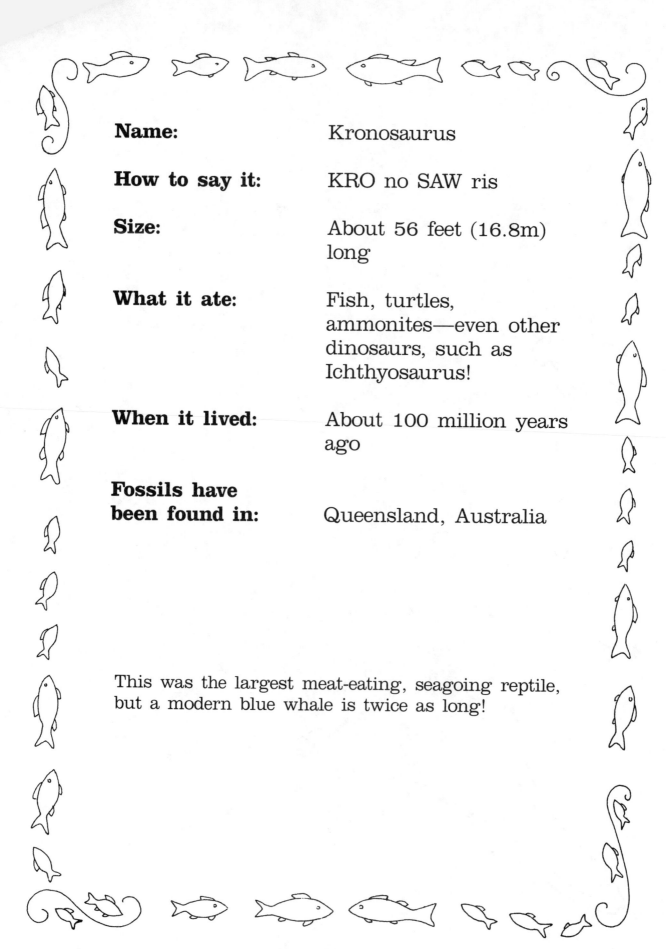

Name:	Kronosaurus
How to say it:	KRO no SAW ris
Size:	About 56 feet (16.8m) long
What it ate:	Fish, turtles, ammonites—even other dinosaurs, such as Ichthyosaurus!
When it lived:	About 100 million years ago
Fossils have been found in:	Queensland, Australia

This was the largest meat-eating, seagoing reptile, but a modern blue whale is twice as long!

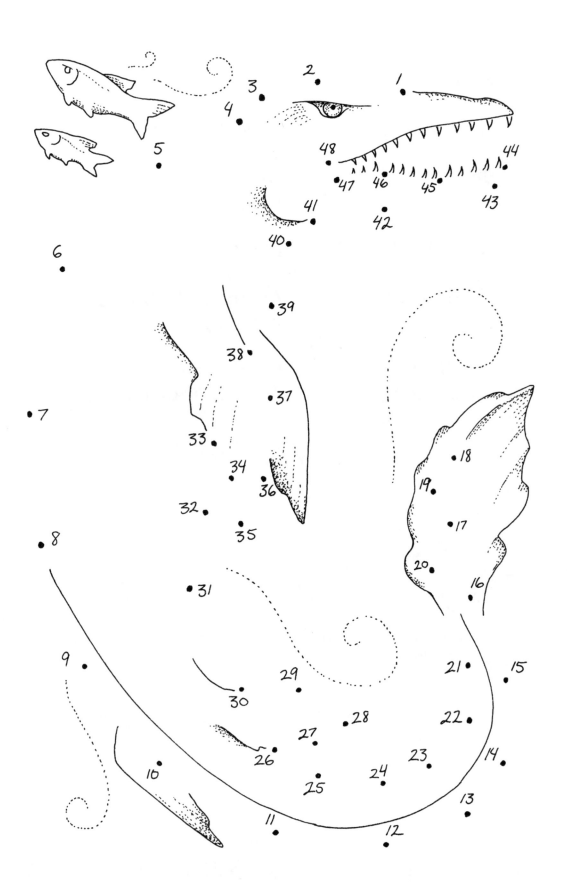

51

Name:	Lambeosaurus
How to say it:	LAM beo SAW ris
Size:	About 40 feet (12m) long
What it ate:	Plants
When it lived:	About 65 to 90 million years ago
Fossils have been found in:	Alberta, Canada

Lambeosaurus probably fed in large herds with other plant-eating dinosaurs.

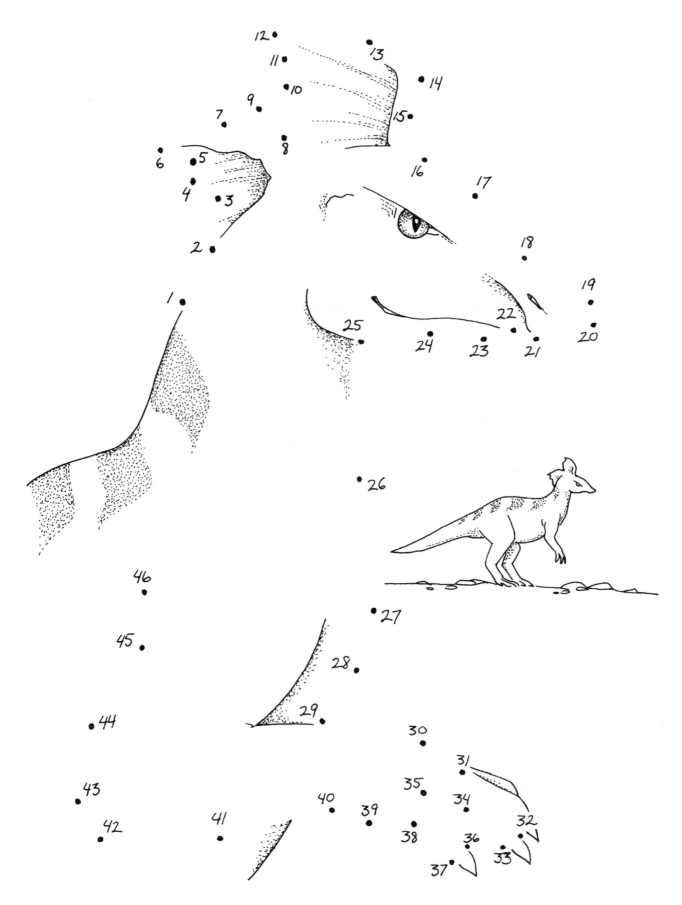

53

Name:	Maiasaura
How to say it:	MY ah SAW rah or mah ee ah SAW rah
Size:	About 25 to 30 feet (7.5–9m) long
What it ate:	Plants
When it lived:	About 80 million years ago
Fossils have been found in:	Montana, U.S.A.

The nests of these dinosaurs have been found with as many as 20 eggs in them.

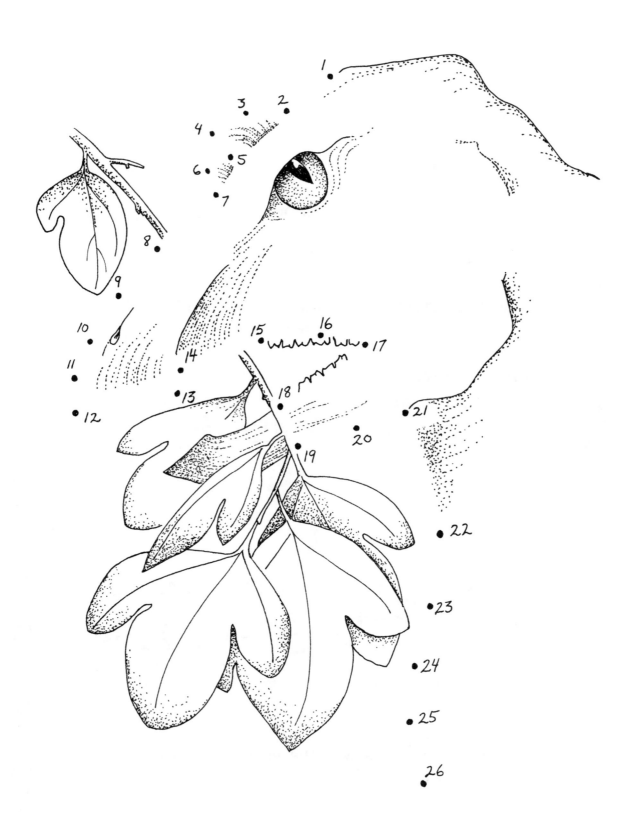

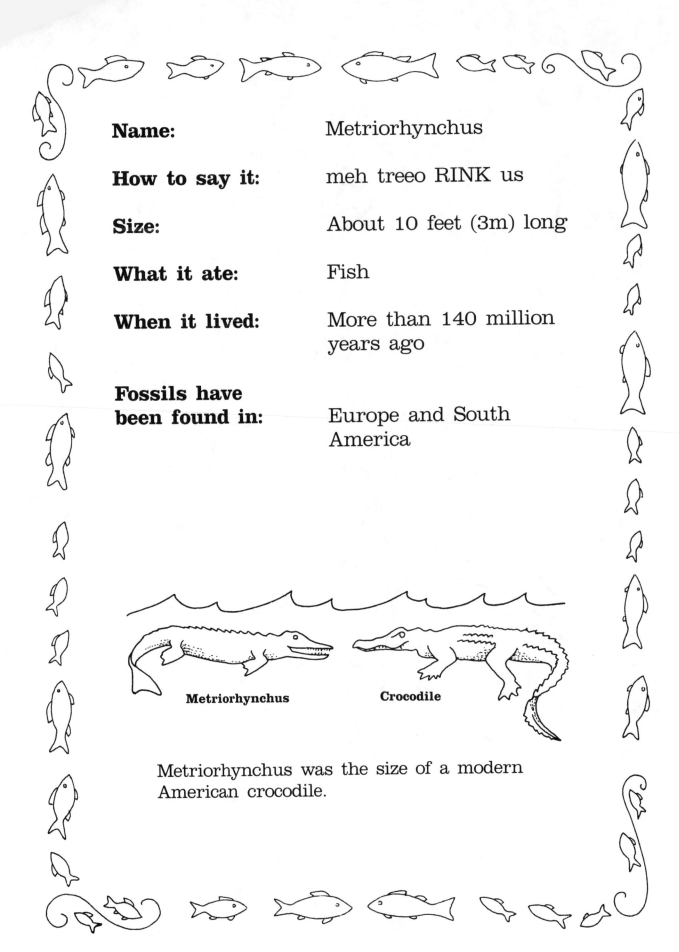

Name: Metriorhynchus

How to say it: meh treeo RINK us

Size: About 10 feet (3m) long

What it ate: Fish

When it lived: More than 140 million years ago

Fossils have been found in: Europe and South America

Metriorhynchus

Crocodile

Metriorhynchus was the size of a modern American crocodile.

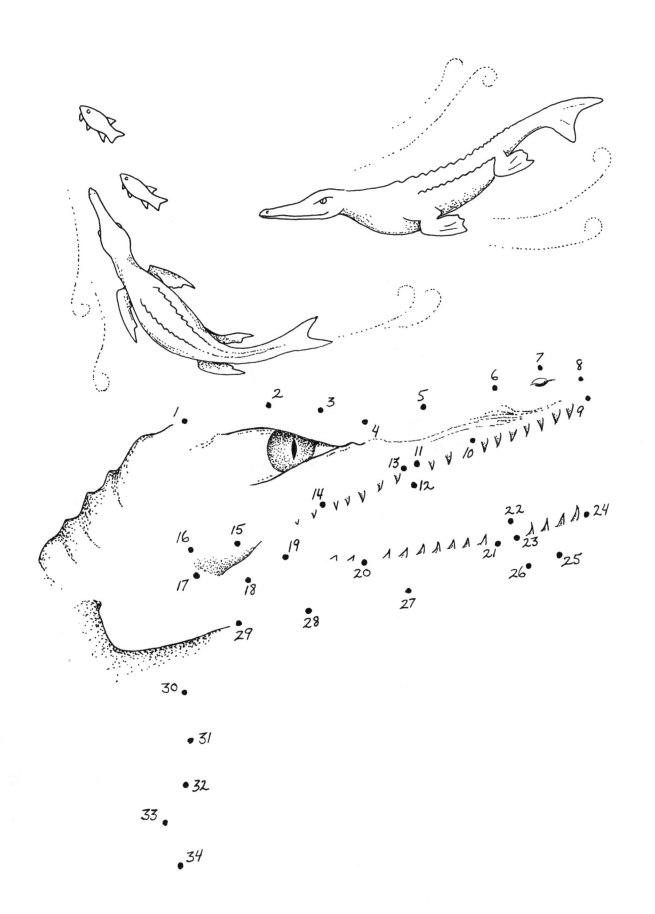

Name:	Monoclonius
How to say it:	monno KLO nee is
Size:	Up to 18 feet (5.4m) long
What it ate:	Plants
When it lived:	About 75 to 80 million years ago
Fossils have been found in:	Montana, U.S.A. Alberta, Canada

Another name for this dinosaur is Centrosaurus (sen tro SAW ris).

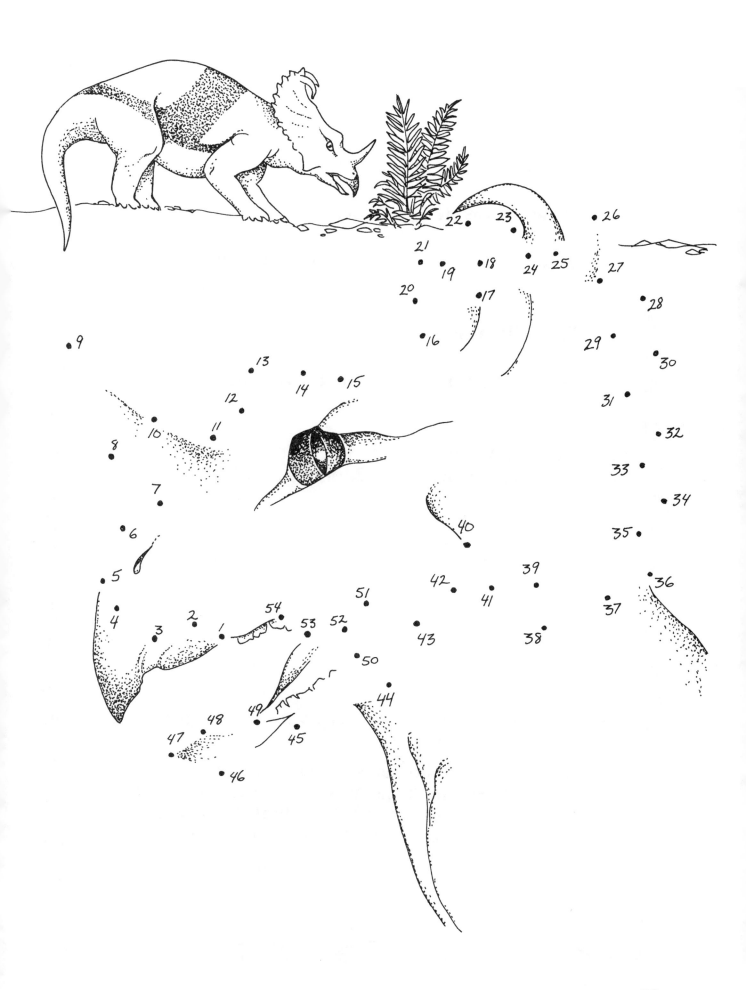

Name:	Orodromeus
How to say it:	orro DRO meeus
Size:	Adults were probably seven feet (2.1m) long.
What it ate:	Plants
When it lived:	About 75 million years ago
Fossils have been found in:	Montana, U.S.A.

This dinosaur is still curled up inside its egg, almost ready to hatch out.

The first person to make a model of Orodromeus was Matt Smith, at the Museum of the Rockies at Montana State University. A medical X-ray scanner was used to find out what was inside the egg.

Orodromeus means "mountain runner" in Greek.

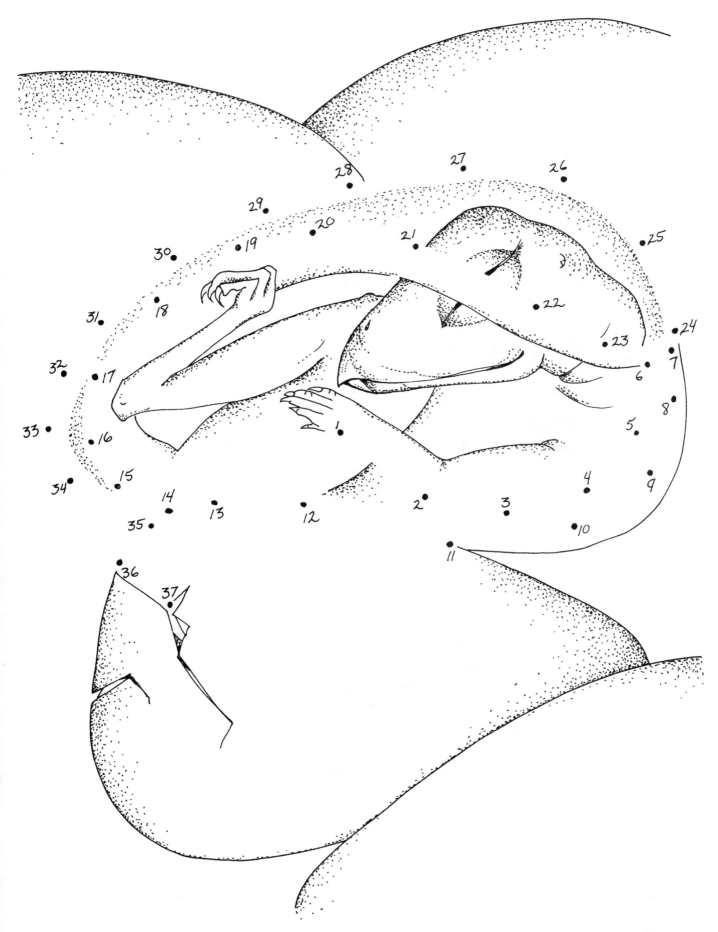

Name:	Oviraptor
How to say it:	OH vih RAP tor
Size:	About 6 to 9 feet (1.8–2.7m) long
What it ate:	Eggs and perhaps some plants
When it lived:	About 70 to 80 million years ago
Fossils have been found in:	The Gobi Desert, Mongolia

Dinosaur names are tricky to say or spell because they come from ancient Greek or Latin words. Sometimes, even scientists don't agree on how to say a name!

Oviraptor means "egg robber" in Latin.

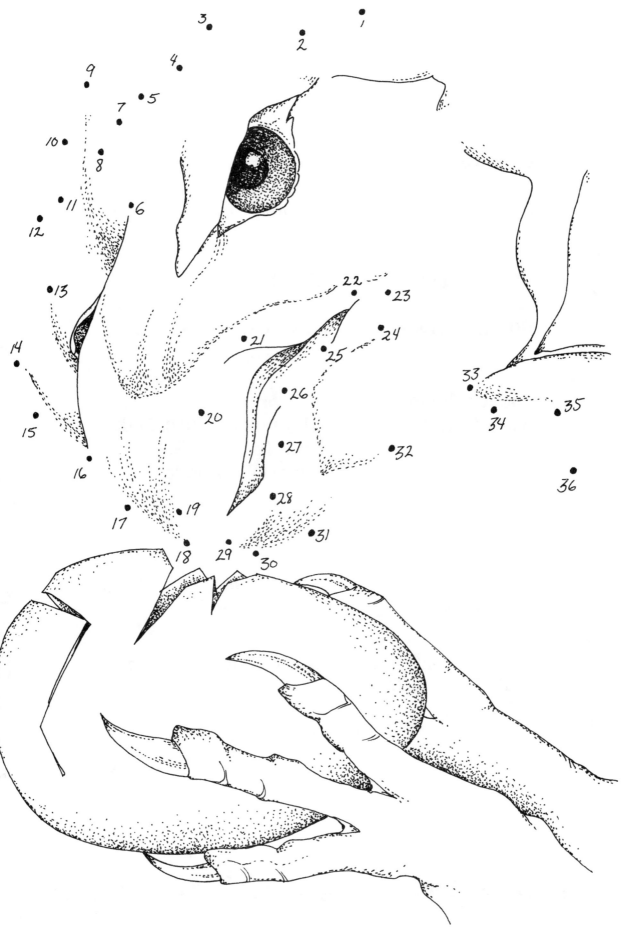

Name:	Panoplosaurus
How to say it:	pan OP loh SAW ris
Size:	About 15 feet (4.5m) long
What it ate:	Plants
When it lived:	About 65 to 80 million years ago
Fossils have been found in:	Montana, South Dakota, and Texas, U.S.A. Alberta, Canada

Some scientists call this dinosaur Paleoscincus (PAIL eeo SKINK us).

Name:	Parasaurolophus
How to say it:	PAIR ah sore OLL uh fis
Size:	About 33 feet (9.9m) long
What it ate:	Plants
When it lived:	About 65 to 80 million years ago
Fossils have been found in:	New Mexico, U.S.A. Alberta, Canada

The long crest on this dinosaur was almost hollow, like a tube. It could have made the voice of the dinosaur sound strange—the way your voice does when you talk into a cardboard tube.

Name:	Plesiosaur
How to say it:	PLEEZ eeo sore
Size:	From 12 to 20 feet (3.6–6m) long
What it ate:	Fish, squid, ammonites
When it lived:	About 200 million years ago
Fossils have been found in:	Wyoming, U.S.A.

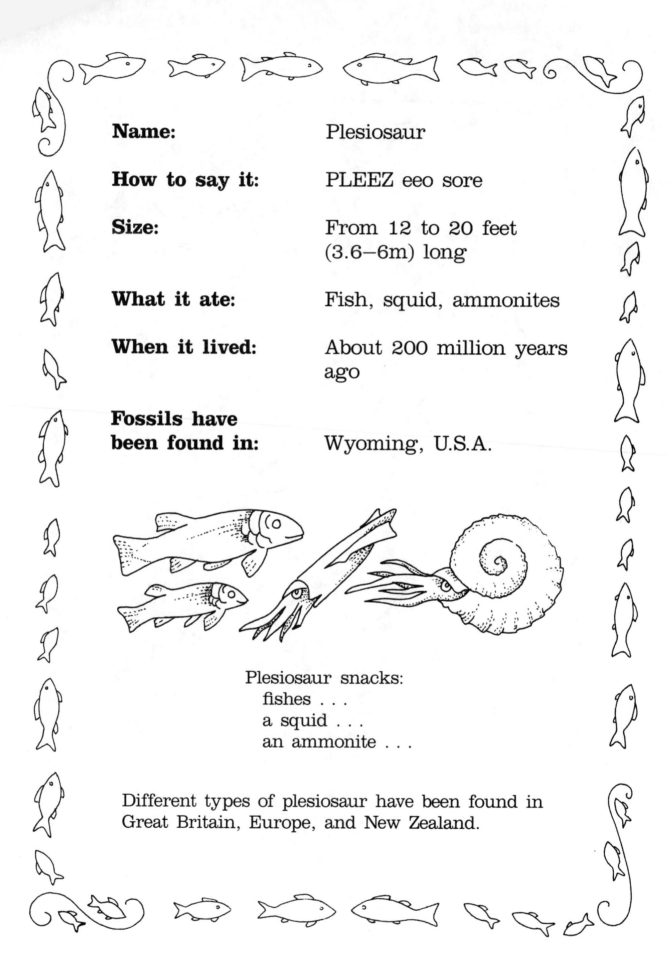

Plesiosaur snacks:
    fishes . . .
    a squid . . .
    an ammonite . . .

Different types of plesiosaur have been found in Great Britain, Europe, and New Zealand.

RUSSO

Name:	Protoceratops
How to say it:	PRO toe SAIR atops
Size:	About 7 feet (2.1m) long
What it ate:	Plants
When it lived:	About 80 million years ago
Fossils have been found in:	The Gobi Desert, Mongolia

Protoceratops may have lived in colonies or small groups.

Name:	Psittacosaurus
How to say it:	SIT ah ko SAW ris
Size:	Nearly seven feet (2.1m) long
What it ate:	Plants
When it lived:	About 95 million years ago
Fossils have been found in:	Mongolia

Fossils of bones do not give any clues to the colors of dinosaurs. Some dinosaurs may have been plain grey like elephants, and others brightly colored like parrots.

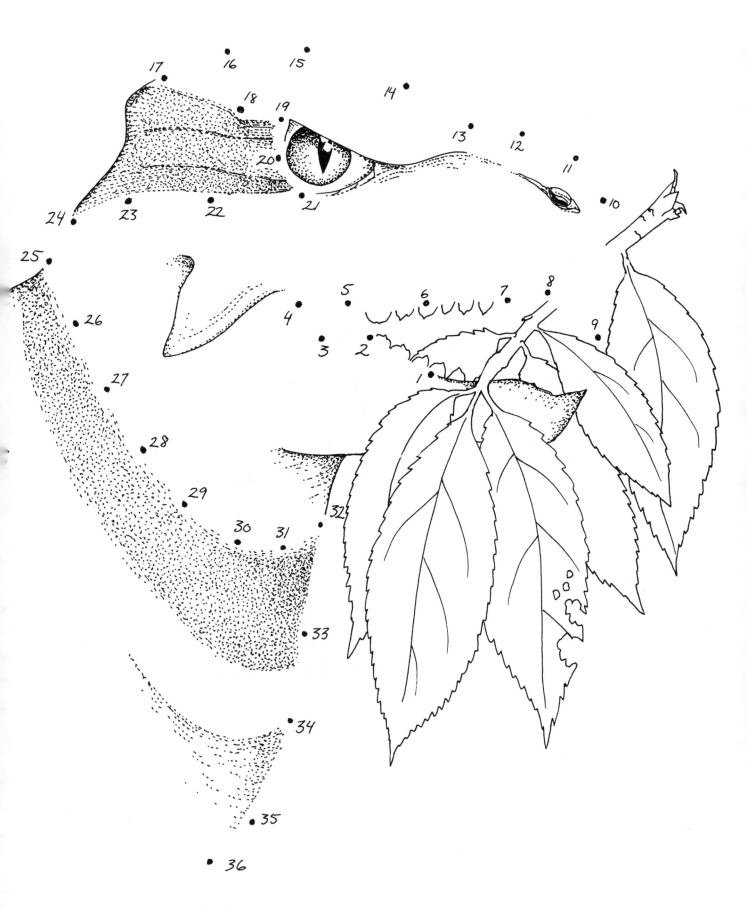

Name:	Pteranodon
How to say it:	ter ANN ah don or TARE anna don
Size:	Wingspan was about 25 feet (7.5m) wide
What it ate:	Fish
When it lived:	About 80 million years ago
Fossils have been found in:	Kansas, U.S.A.

Pteranodon probably couldn't flap its wings, but it might have been able to glide.

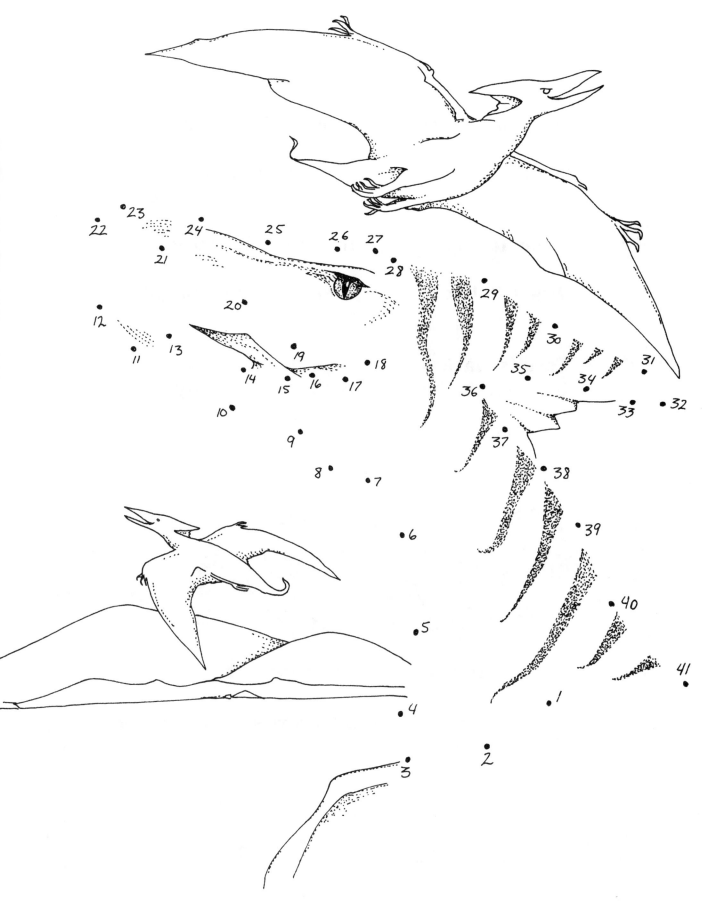

Name:	Pterodactylus
How to say it:	terra DAK till us
Size:	Wingspan of about 18 inches (45 cm) across
What it ate:	Insects, fish, worms
When it lived:	About 150 million years ago
Fossils have been found in:	Bavaria, Germany

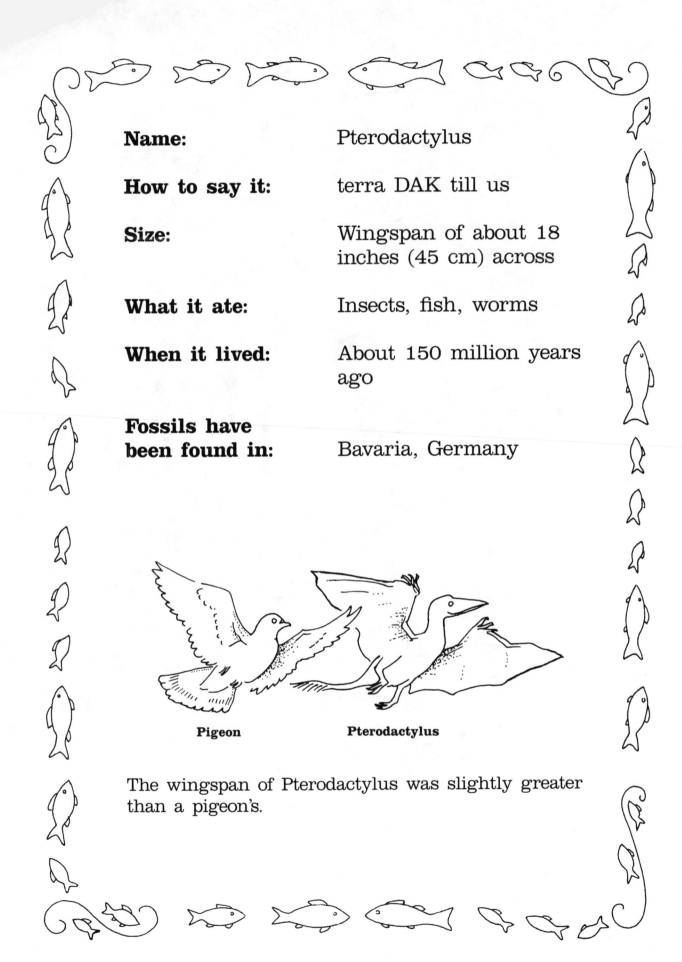

Pigeon   Pterodactylus

The wingspan of Pterodactylus was slightly greater than a pigeon's.

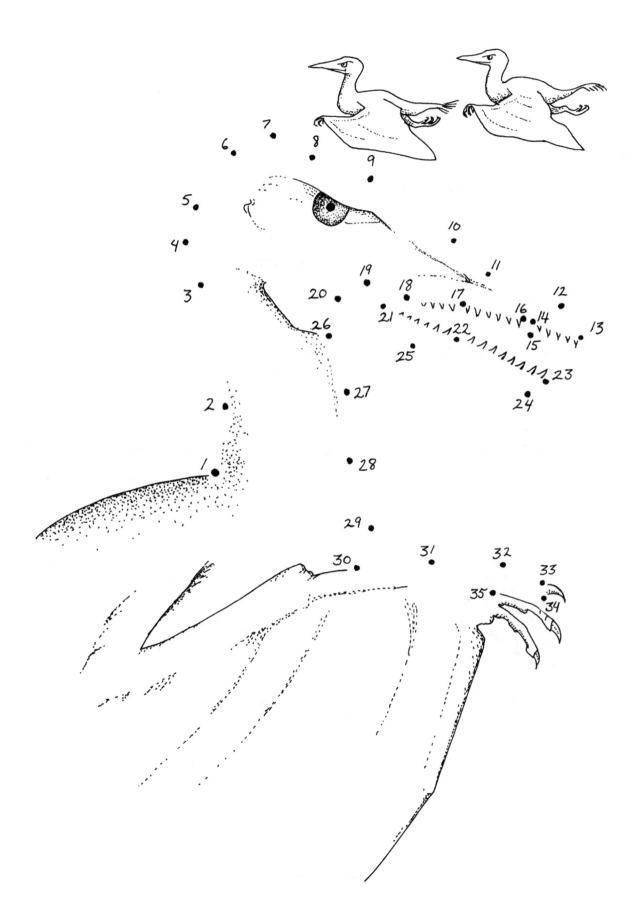

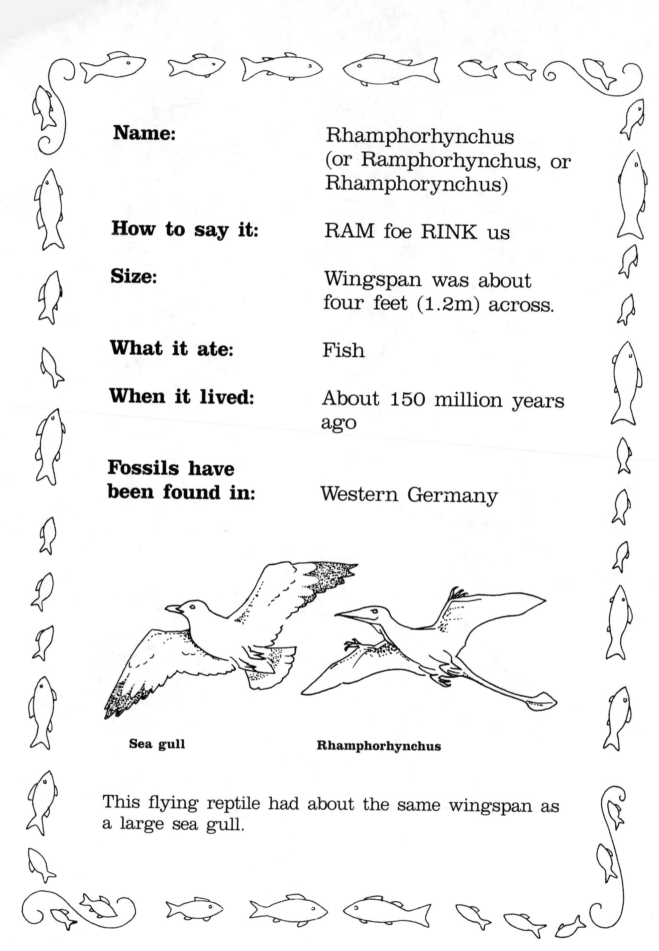

Name:	Rhamphorhynchus (or Ramphorhynchus, or Rhamphorynchus)
How to say it:	RAM foe RINK us
Size:	Wingspan was about four feet (1.2m) across.
What it ate:	Fish
When it lived:	About 150 million years ago
Fossils have been found in:	Western Germany

Sea gull   **Rhamphorhynchus**

This flying reptile had about the same wingspan as a large sea gull.

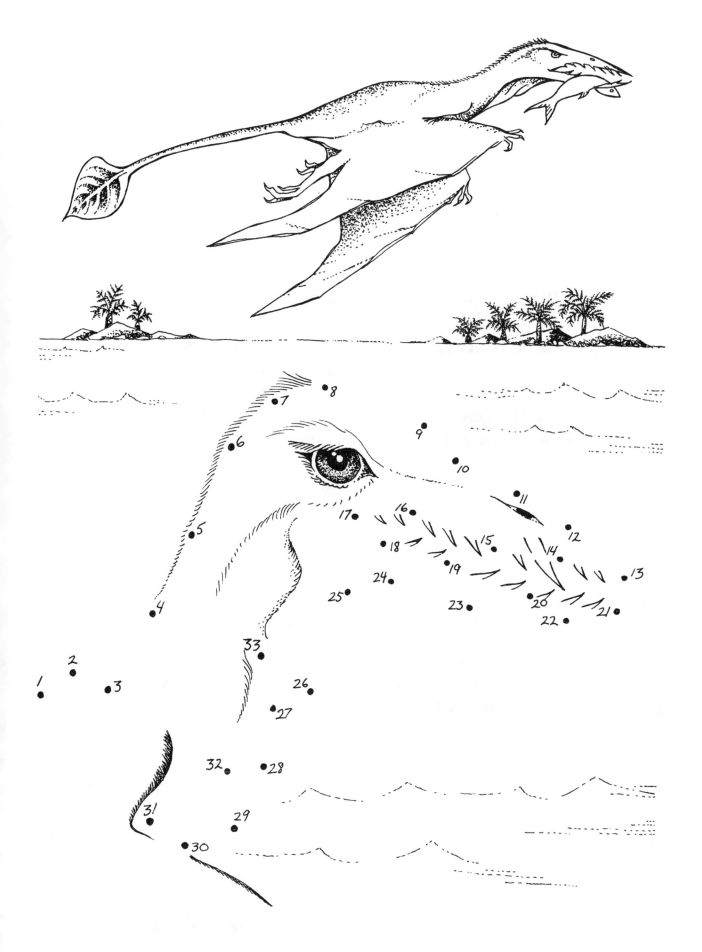

Name:	Scutellosaurus
How to say it:	SKU tello SAW ris
Size:	About five feet (1.5m) long
What it ate:	Plants
When it lived:	Nearly 200 million years ago
Fossils have been found in:	Arizona, U.S.A.

This dinosaur is named for its "scutes," the hard bony plates on its back.

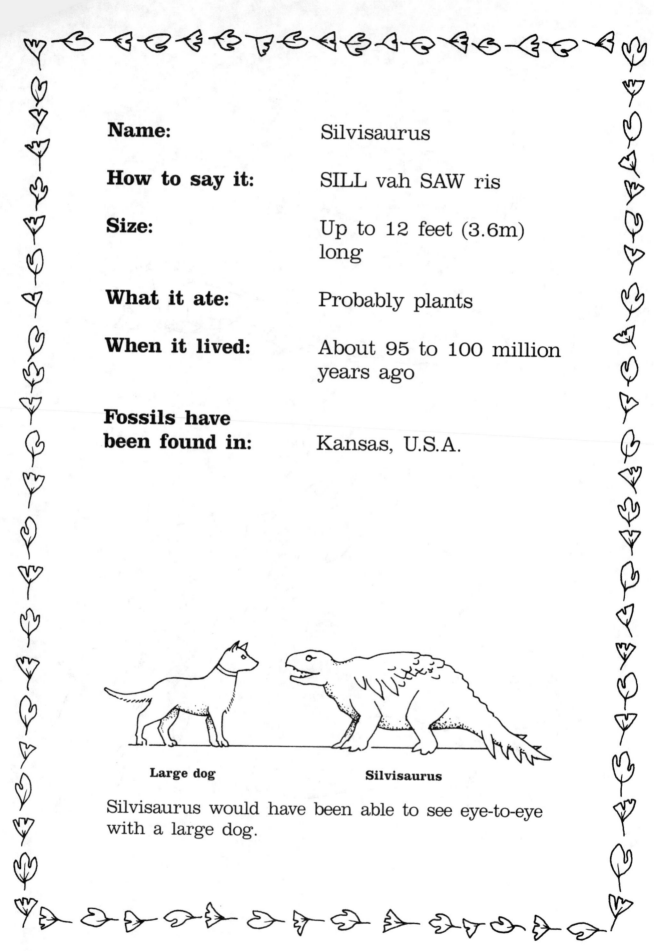

Name:	Silvisaurus
How to say it:	SILL vah SAW ris
Size:	Up to 12 feet (3.6m) long
What it ate:	Probably plants
When it lived:	About 95 to 100 million years ago
Fossils have been found in:	Kansas, U.S.A.

Large dog   **Silvisaurus**

Silvisaurus would have been able to see eye-to-eye with a large dog.

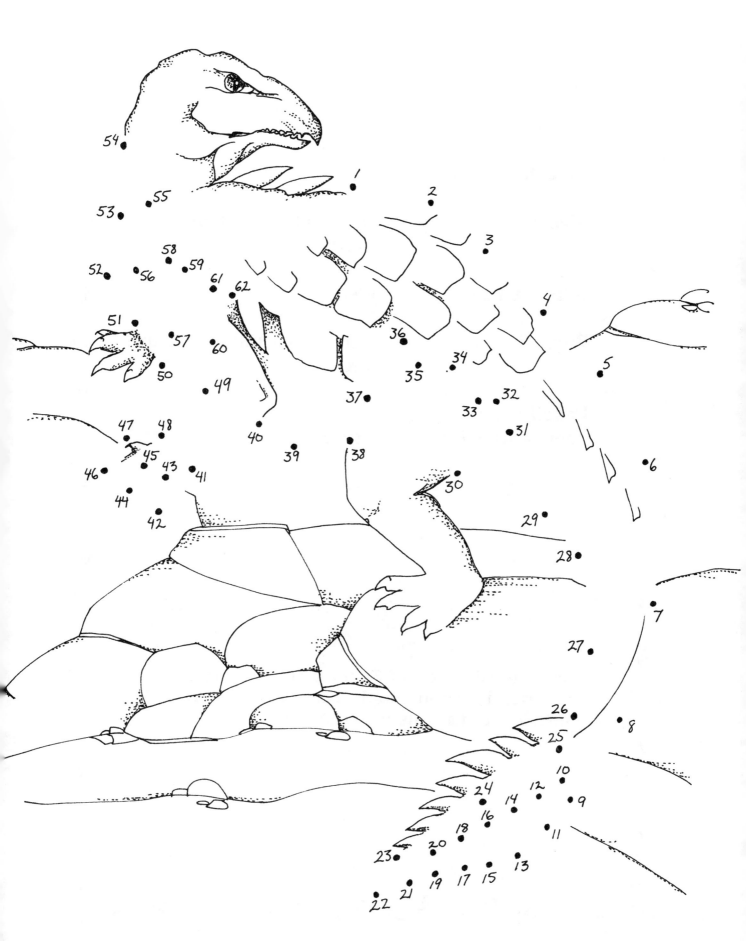

83

Name:	Spinosaurus
How to say it:	SPY no SAW ris
Size:	Up to 50 feet (1.5m) long
What it ate:	Meat
When it lived:	About 110 million years ago
Fossils have been found in:	Egypt

The original fossils of Spinosaurus were lost or destroyed in World War II. Scientists hope to find another set of fossils in the future.

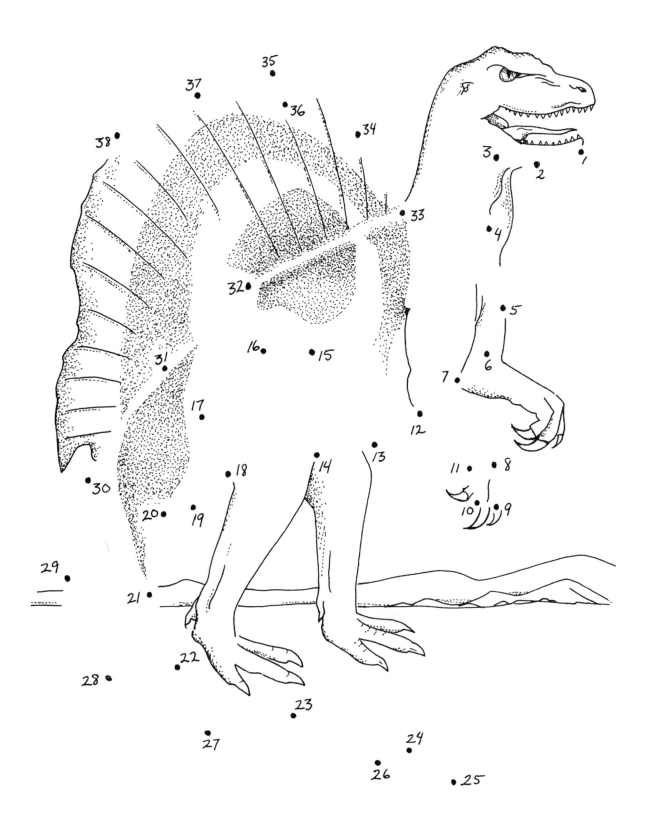

Name:	Stegoceras
How to say it:	steg OSS uh ris
Size:	About 6 feet (1.8m) long
What it ate:	Plants
When it lived:	About 65 to 80 million years ago
Fossils have been found in:	Alberta, Canada

Stegoceras belong to a group known as "bone-heads" or "dome-heads." These dinosaurs have thick, bony skulls.

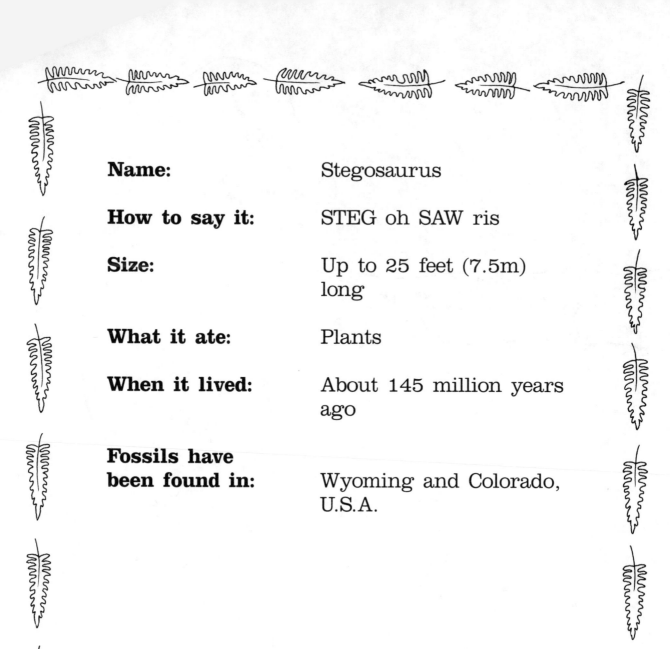

Name:	Stegosaurus
How to say it:	STEG oh SAW ris
Size:	Up to 25 feet (7.5m) long
What it ate:	Plants
When it lived:	About 145 million years ago
Fossils have been found in:	Wyoming and Colorado, U.S.A.

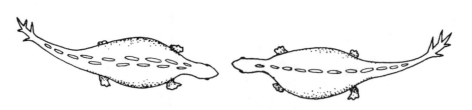

Were the plates on this dinosaur's back arranged in one row or two?

Most scientists think it was an uneven row of two.

Name:	Triceratops
How to say it:	try SAIR atops
Size:	Up to 30 feet (9m) long
	It weighed as much as a modern elephant.
What it ate:	Plants
When it lived:	About 70 million years ago
Fossils have been found in:	Wyoming and Montana, U.S.A. Alberta and Saskatchewan, Canada

Ten different types of Triceratops have been found in the American West.

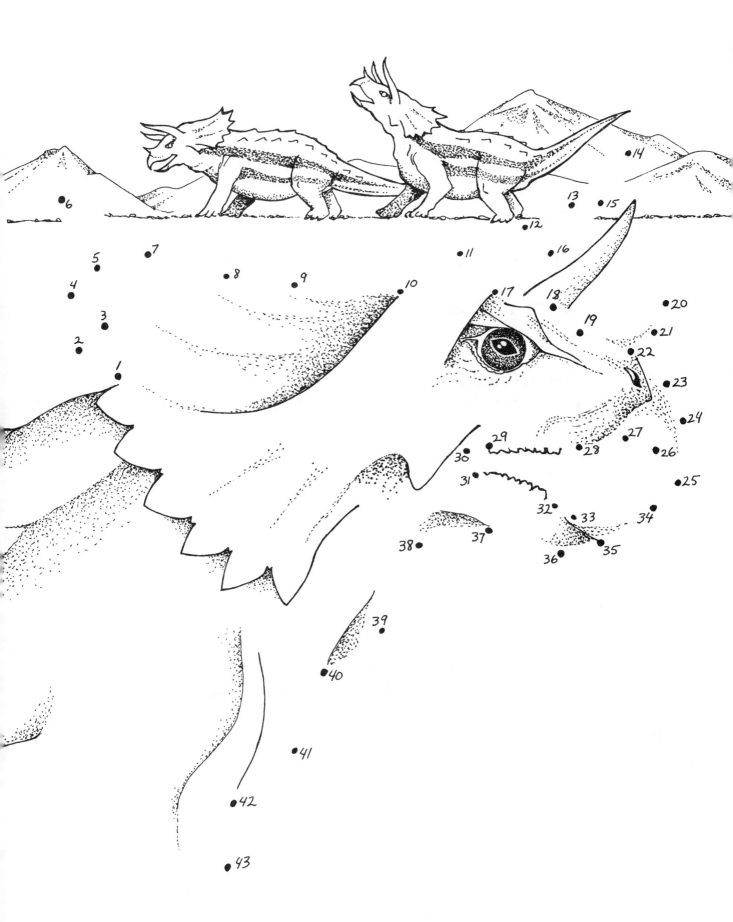

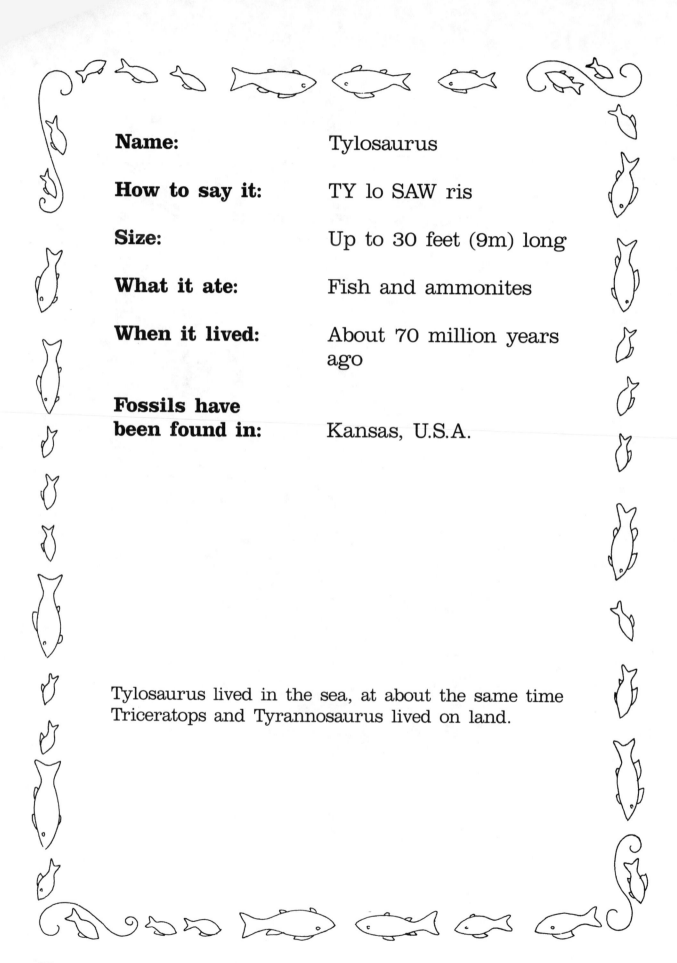

Name:	Tylosaurus
How to say it:	TY lo SAW ris
Size:	Up to 30 feet (9m) long
What it ate:	Fish and ammonites
When it lived:	About 70 million years ago
Fossils have been found in:	Kansas, U.S.A.

Tylosaurus lived in the sea, at about the same time Triceratops and Tyrannosaurus lived on land.

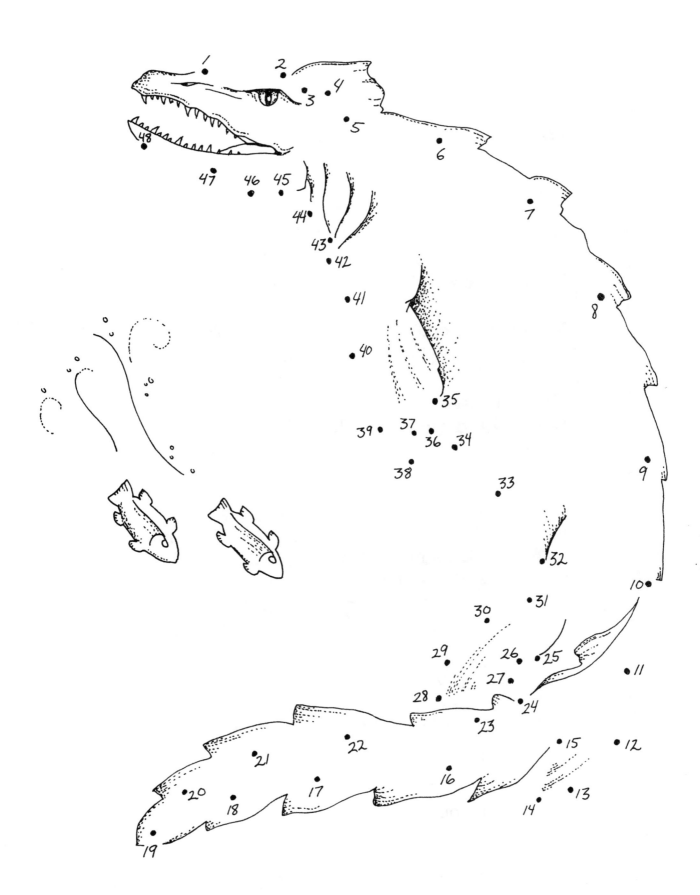

93

Name:	Tyrannosaurus
How to say it:	ty RAN ah SAW ris
Size:	Up to 50 feet (15m) long
	About 20 feet (6m) tall
What it ate:	Meat
When it lived:	About 65 to 70 million years ago
Fossils have been found in:	Hell Creek, Montana, U.S.A.

Some scientists think Tyrannosaurus weighed as little as two and a half tons (2.25 tonnes), while others think he might have weighed as much as seven tons (6.3 tonnes).

The largest teeth of Tyrannosaurus were longer than a ball-point pen.

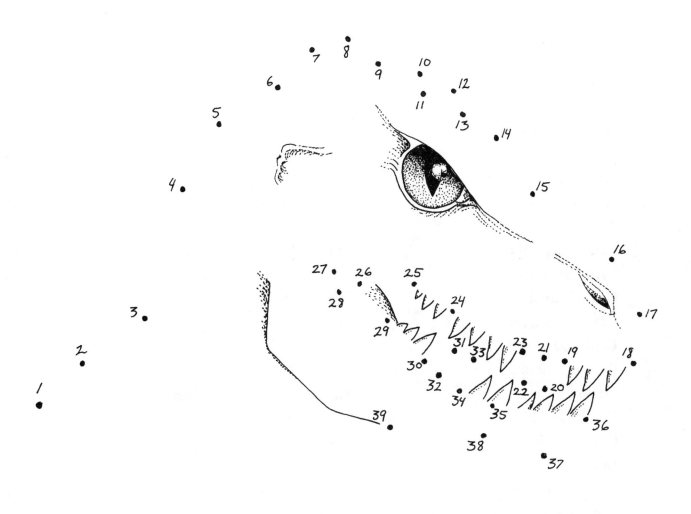
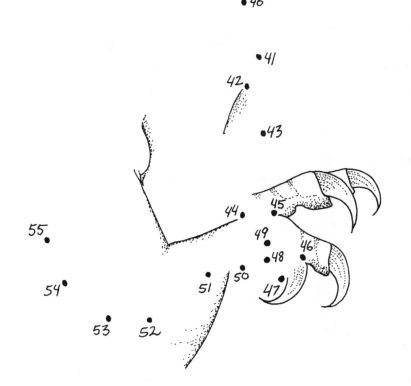

95

Contents/Index

About the Creatures in This Book	3	Herrerasaurus	42
Acknowledgments	2	Hypacrosaurus	44
Albertosaurus	4	Hypsilophodon	46
Allosaurus	6	Ichthyosaurus	48
Apatosaurus	8	Kronosaurus	50
Archaeopteryx	10	Lambeosaurus	52
Bone-heads	86	Maiasaura	54
Brachiosaurus	12	Metriorhynchus	56
Brontosaurus	8	Monoclonius	58
Carnotaurus	14	Orodromeus	60
Carnotosaurus	14	Oviraptor	62
Centrosaurus	58	*Paleoscincus*	64
Ceratosaurus	16	Panoplosaurus	64
Coelophysis	18	Parasaurolophus	66
Compsognathus	20	Plesiosaur	68
Corythosaurus	22	Protoceratops	70
Deinonychus	24	Psittacosaurus	72
Dilophosaurus	26	Pteranodon	74
Dimetrodon	28	Pterodactylus	76
Dimorphodon	30	Rhamphorhynchus	78
Diplodocus	32	Scutellosaurus	80
Dome-heads	86	Silvisaurus	82
Edmontosaurus	34	Spinosaurus	84
Euoplocephalus	36	Stegoceras	86
First Bird	10	Stegosaurus	88
Gallimimus	38	Triceratops	90, 92
Garudimimus	40	Tylosaurus	92
Gorgosaurus	4	Tyrannosaurus	4, 92, 94

Note: Some dinosaurs have been known by other names. These other names are listed in italics.

$5.95
Can. $8.95

DINOSAUR
DOTS

Connect the dots and find a dinosaur! Then take some crayons and color it in.

You'll meet 30 amazing beasts and find out all about them too. You'll even learn how to say their weird names—like:

- Albertosaurus (al BER toe SAW ris)
- Ichthyosaurus (IK theeo SAW ris)
- Stegosaurus (STEG oh SAW ris)

And best of all, you'll have a whole lot of fun making new friends that are millions and millions and millions of years old!

Sterling Publishing Co., Inc.
New York

ISBN 0-8069-7388-9

90000

9 780806 973883

0 49725 07388 3

TEACHER'S GUIDE

English, Yes!

Learning English Through Literature

BK00655174

Level 3: Beginning